This Bing book belongs to:

. . . .

Copyright © 2015 Acamar Films Ltd

First published in the UK in 2015 by HarperCollins *Children's Books*,
a division of HarperCollins Publishers Ltd, 1 London Bridge Street, London SE1 9GF.

1 3 5 7 9 10 8 6 4 2

ISBN: 978-0-00-758102-3

Based on the script by Lead Writer: Denise Cassar and Team Writers: Lucy Murphy, Ted Dewan and Mikael Shields.

Adapted from the original books by Ted Dewan and using images created by Acamar Films, Brown Bag Films and Tandem Ltd.

Edited by Neil Dunnicliffe.

Designed by Anna Lubecka.

www.harpercollins.co.uk

Printed in Italy

Bing™

Big Slide

HarperCollins *Children's Books*

Round the corner, not far away,
there's something new for Bing today.

Bing and Flop are at the park
with Bing's friend, Pando.

"LOOK!"

"WOW!"

It's a brand new
climbing frame.

"It's got a **slide!**" says Bing.
"...and a **tunnel!**" calls Pando.
"...and a **bridge!**"

"Come on, Bing!" says Pando.

"Wait for me…" shouts Bing.

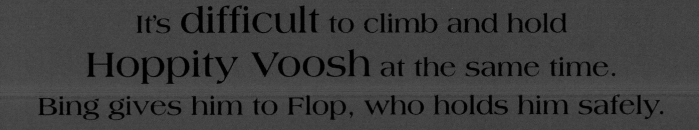

It's **difficult** to climb and hold
Hoppity Voosh at the same time.
Bing gives him to Flop, who holds him safely.

Bing follows Pando through the tunnel. It's very **tippy**!

"Come on, Bing!" laughs Pando. "It goes this way."

"Did you see me, Flop?" shouts Bing.

"Yup, I saw you," calls Flop, "and so did Hoppity!"

Next it's the **rope ladder**. Pando climbs up quickly. "Come on, Bing!"

Bing grabs hold of the ropes. "Ooh, it's all **boingy**!" Bravely, he climbs to the top.

Pando dances across the wobbly bridge.

"Woohoo! Wobbly wobbly!"

Bing steps on to
the bridge. It's
very wobbly.
He carefully makes
his way across.

"Did you see
me, Flop?" he calls.

"Yup. You OK
up there?"

"Yup. I'm OK."

Finally, they reach the slide.
"Woooah, look Bing!"

Pando goes first.

"Look at me! Here... I...
gooooOOOO!"

Whoosh! Pando whizzes down the slide.

"Me next!" says Bing. He bounds to the **edge.**

"Woah!"

The slide is **high.**

Very high.

Scared, Bing jumps back.

"Flop!"

"What's up Bing?"

"It's too high."

Flop asks if he should come up.
"Yup. Can you bring Hoppity?"

Flop quickly makes his way up to Bing.

Meanwhile, Pando goes down the slide **again**.

"Here... I... goooooooooo!"

Flop reaches the top of the slide. He hands Hoppity to Bing, who hugs him tight.

"So, you did the **steps**," says Flop.

"Mmm," says Bing.

"And then the **tippy tunnel**."

"Yup."

"And then the boingy rope ladder."

"Yup."

"So, what's next?"

Bing points to the slide. "But it's too **high**."

Meanwhile, Pando is about to **whizz** down the slide **again**.

Flop says, "How about we **watch** how Pando does it **one more time**, so we know what to do?"

"Don't be scared," says Pando,
"you do it **like this**." He **bounces**
forward, holding on to the handles.

"Here... I... goOOOOOOOO!"

"It looks like fun," says Flop. "Shall we let Hoppity go first?"

"Mmmm. OK."

Bing carries Hoppity over to the top of the slide.

"Ready, Hoppity?

Here... I... goooooooo!"

Whoosh! Pando catches
Hoppity as he reaches
the bottom.

"Ha ha, he
liked it!"
laughs Bing.

Now it's Bing's turn. Slowly he sits at the top of the slide.

"Look at me, Flop.
Here... I... goooooooo!"

Whoosh! Bing launches
himself down the slide.
"Woo-hooooooo!"

"Did you see me, Flop?" asks Bing.
"Yup, I saw you. Good for you, Bing Bunny."

"Let's do it again!"

Hi!

Me and Pando found a **new** thing at the park.

It had a **climby** bit,

and a **tippy** bit,

and a **wobbly** bit, and it was **fun**.

But then it had a very high slide... and that was scary,

so Pando showed us, and Hoppity went first.

If you're scared of something you can watch someone else do it. And if they like it, you might like it too.

Going down the big slide...

it's a Bing thing!